Marky Polo's Travels
Marky Polo in Běijīng

WRITTEN BY **EMILY LIM-LEH** • ILLUSTRATED BY **NICHOLAS LIEM**

WS Education

NEW JERSEY • LONDON • SINGAPORE • BEIJING • SHANGHAI • HONG KONG • TAIPEI • CHENNAI • TOKYO

A Guide to Experiencing Augmented Reality in This Book

1. 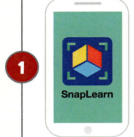 Download SnapLearn app.

2.  Activate by scanning this book's barcode. Then, tap on the book cover image on your screen.

3.  Scan and hold camera over scanned page to see AR. Wherever you see this icon, scan the whole page.

SnapLearn is compatible with devices running minimally on iOS 8 and Android 5.0 with gyroscope. For the best AR experience, please scan the physical or PDF version of the book. For any app-related issues, please contact us via email at hello@snaplearn.com.

Powered By: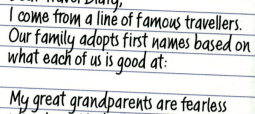

Dear Travel Diary,

I come from a line of famous travellers. Our family adopts first names based on what each of us is good at:

My great grandparents are fearless adventurer Macho Polo and top martial arts fighter Muay Thai Polo.

My grandparents are Matcha and Miso Polo, top experts on Japanese tea and seasoning.

My parents are Masala and Mala Polo, largest collectors of spices in the world.

My cousin Martial Polo heard about my first overseas trip to Tokyo. She's invited me to visit her in Beijing!

Marky Polo
(Trying to make my mark in the world... Mark my words, I will discover what I am good at!)

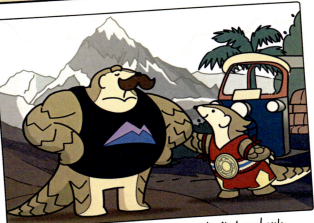

Great-grandfather **Macho Polo** — the first and only pangolin to scale to the top of Mount Everest. He met his match in great-grandmother **Muay Thai Polo**, top martial arts fighter from Thailand.

Grandfather **Matcha Polo** and grandmother **Miso Polo** discovered their love for Japan when they travelled there. Matcha Polo became an expert in green tea and Miso Polo an expert in Japanese food seasoning.

Father **Masala Polo** travelled to India and built up the largest spice collection in the world there. Mother **Mala Polo** shares his love of spices, but of the spicy, Sichuan tongue-numbing kind, from her China travels.

Martial Polo — disciple of Chinese martial arts.

Marky Polo — Travelling out of Singapore for the second time... Will I leave my mark on China?

Marky Polo the pangolin was happy to arrive in Beijing. He had not seen Martial Polo since her visit to Singapore a long time ago.

"欢迎! Welcome!" Martial said. "Come, let's head home."
Martial marched off at full speed. Marky hurried after his cousin.

"Wait! Aren't we going into your home?" Marky asked.

"No way! We have lots to see and do," Martial said.
"Uncle, please go to Beijing Olympic Park!" Martial told the taxi driver.

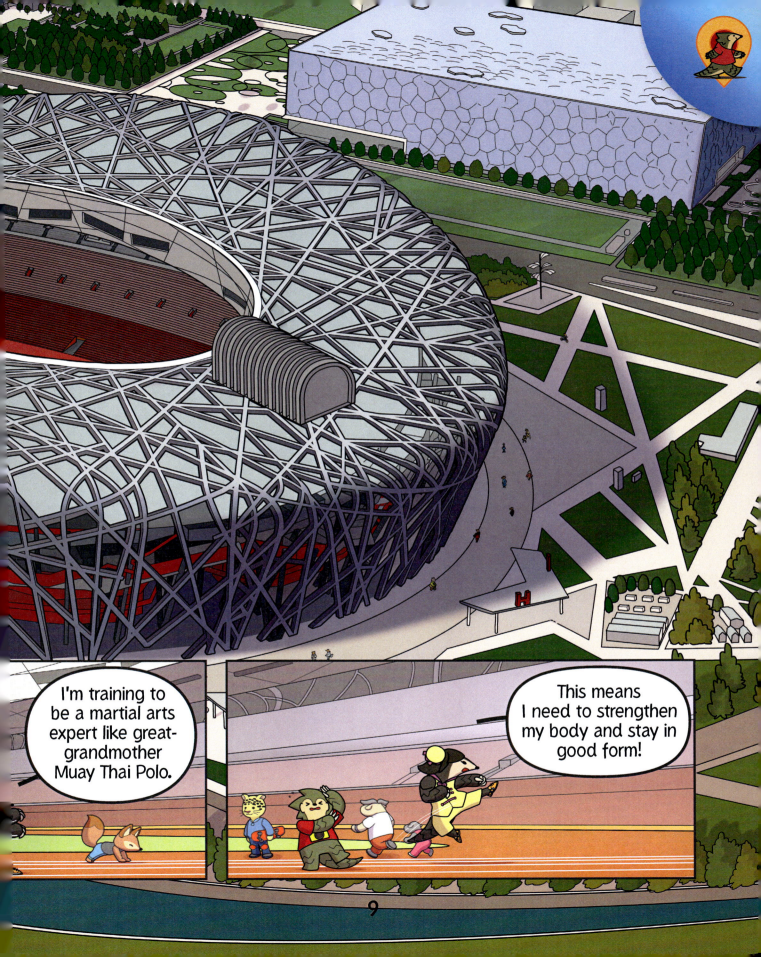

The Summer Palace, a UNESCO World Heritage Site, is said to be the best-preserved imperial garden in the world, and the largest of its kind in China. It was also the residence of Empress Dowager Cixi, the most famous and influential Chinese empress.

The Great Wall of China is the largest man-made project in the world. Built for defence reasons, it stretches over 21,000 km across deserts, grasslands and mountains from the west to the east of China. It is a UNESCO World Heritage Site.

Martial sprinted up the steps. "Last one to reach the top is a rotten ant!" she yelled.

Marky panted as he tried to keep up.

Martial sped down the length of the wall.

Wait for me!

Quick! Faster!

I need a holiday from this holiday.

When Marky finally caught up with Martial, she was tapping her watch impatiently. "We are behind schedule. We will take the Mutianyu Toboggan Ride down."

Martial pushed him into a toboggan car. "I'll be right behind you," she said.

By the time they returned to the car, Marky's scales were quivering.

"Next stop: Forbidden City!" Martial announced.

Martial and Marky jogged past the Gate of Heavenly Peace at Tiananmen.

They dashed through the outer court where the emperors had held ceremonies.

They scurried around the inner court where the emperors had slept.

They bolted across the Imperial Garden where the emperors had relaxed.

"I'm tired and hungry," Marky grumbled as his tummy growled.

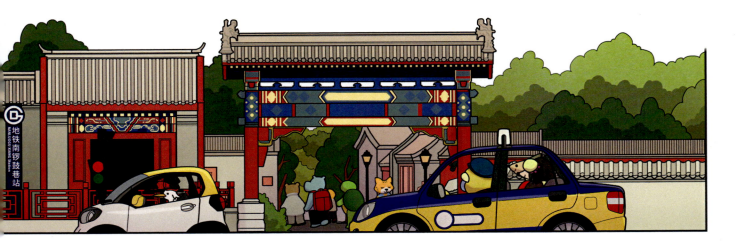

"Kung fu disciples must practise self-control and not give in so easily to such needs," Martial scolded. "Let's walk through the *hutong* first."

Hutong refers to a narrow lane, alley, or small street between rows of single-storey buildings in olden day Beijing.

"Last one to reach the end is a rotten termite... **oof!**" Martial cried as she tripped.

"Oh no... are you okay?" Marky said.

"I think I sprained my ankle," Martial said.

"I'll look for a clinic so we can get your ankle checked," Marky said and he rolled off speedily.

Marky returned swiftly and helped Martial to walk to a traditional Chinese medicine clinic that he found.

The doctor examined Martial's ankle.

"Kung fu isn't only about pushing your body hard and building muscle strength," the doctor said.

"Then, what is it?" Martial asked.

"You need to strike a harmonious balance, like Yin and Yang," the doctor explained.

"For example, Yin can represent how you control your breathing, qi and mind. Then, Yang represents your external muscle strength. I see many new kung fu students who injure themselves because they only focus on building physical strength."

"How about lunch now?"

"Yum... the food seems to taste better when we eat unhurriedly."

"It sure does! You know, chewing slowly takes discipline," Marky said with a wink.

Martial slowed down for the rest of Marky's visit.

They watched a theatre show about a young boy who wanted to become a kung fu master.

They saw another action-packed show with flying acrobats.

Marky and Martial were both happy to experience all the action from the comfort of their seats.

I'm enjoying taking it slow. Maybe I should switch to tai chi instead!

We took our time to visit these cool places and enjoy popular activities in Beijing:

At Tiananmen Square

Eating Peking duck

At Happy Valley Beijing

At China Science and Technology Museum

Chang'an Boulevard

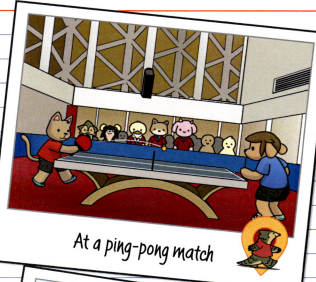
At a ping-pong match

At the Temple of Heaven

At the National Centre for the Performing Arts

At 798 Art Zone

Watching Beijing opera

Fun facts on some animals native to China:

See if you can spot these local animals in the story!

Giant panda

The giant panda is a national treasure in China. This endearing animal lives in the mountains of central China amidst bamboo forests. It feeds primarily on bamboo and needs at least 28 pounds of it to meet its daily needs. It can spend up to 16 hours a day eating.

Red panda

The red panda is about the size of a house cat. It appears related to weasels, raccoons, and skunks. 90% of its time is spent up in trees to avoid predators. The red panda lives in the chilly mountains of central China, Nepal and Myanmar. It uses its bushy tail as a blanket to keep warm.

Clouded leopard

The clouded leopard is named after the distinctive 'clouds' on its coat. It is a very good climber and spends most of its life up in trees. It has the longest canine teeth relative to body size in any cat, hence its nickname of 'modern-day sabre-tooth'. The clouded leopard is found in the mountains of southern China and the Himalayan region as well as Southeast Asia.

Mandarin duck

The colourful mandarin duck is known as a 'perching duck', as it has the unique ability to perch high in trees. It nests in holes in trees, sometimes faraway from the water. This species is found in China and North Asia.

Golden snub-nosed monkey

The golden snub-nosed monkey, also known as the Sichuan snub-nosed monkey, is a very rare species found only in central and southwest China. It can live in extremely cold temperatures, where no other non-human primates can survive.

It has a unique 'snub' nose which has no protruding nasal bones, which may help protect it from frostbite.

Now, let's learn more about the Chinese pangolin:

Martial Polo is a Chinese pangolin, once found in forests and grasslands across southern China and other parts of Asia. In China, the pangolin is also called *ling-li*, meaning 'hill carp', due to its brownish-yellow scales resembling those of Chinese carp.

The Chinese pangolin is a shy, slow-moving creature. Its diet consists primarily of ants and termites. Like its pangolin relatives, the Chinese pangolin curls up tightly into a scaly ball when threatened. Pangolins are critically endangered as they are the world's most trafficked animal.

For Caleb, who inspires me with fun, comic ideas for Marky Polo's Travels
—E.L.L.

For the little ones who love to explore, dream and discover
—N.L.

Published by
WS Education, an imprint of
World Scientific Publishing Co. Pte. Ltd.
5 Toh Tuck Link, Singapore 596224
USA office: 27 Warren Street, Suite 401-402, Hackensack, NJ 07601
UK office: 57 Shelton Street, Covent Garden, London WC2H 9HE

National Library Board, Singapore Cataloguing in Publication Data
Name(s): Lim, Emily, 1971– | Liem, Nicholas, illustrator.
Title: Marky Polo in Beijing / written by Emily Lim-Leh ; illustrated by Nicholas Liem.
Other Title(s): Marky Polo's Travels ; Volume 2.
Description: Singapore : WS Education, [2021]
Identifier(s): ISBN 978-981-12-4435-3 (hardcover) | 978-981-12-4540-4 (paperback) |
    978-981-12-4436-0 (ebook for institutions) | 978-981-12-4437-7 (ebook for individuals)
Subject(s): LCSH: Martial arts--Juvenile fiction. | Beijing (China)--Juvenile fiction.
Classification: DDC 428.6--dc23

British Library Cataloguing-in-Publication Data
A catalogue record for this book is available from the British Library.

Text copyright © 2022 by Emily Lim-Leh
Illustration copyright © 2022 by Nicholas Liem

Copyright © 2022 by World Scientific Publishing Co. Pte. Ltd.
All rights reserved. This book, or parts thereof, may not be reproduced in any form or by any means, electronic or mechanical, including photocopying, recording or any information storage and retrieval system now known or to be invented, without written permission from the publisher.

For photocopying of material in this volume, please pay a copying fee through the Copyright Clearance Center, Inc., 222 Rosewood Drive, Danvers, MA 01923, USA. In this case permission to photocopy is not required from the publisher.

Desk Editor: Daniele Lee

Printed in Singapore

Look out for more dynamic, full-colour illustrated children's books in this exciting series *Marky Polo's Travels*. **Enriched by Augmented Reality, Marky Polo takes on Singapore next!**

To receive updates about children's titles from WS Education, go to https://www.worldscientific.com/page/newsletter/ subscribe, choose "Education", click on "Children's Books" and key in your email address.